Little Lamb Lost

David Bedford

Illustrated by **Karen Sapp**

QEB Publishing

Little Lamb was warm in the sun
with his big sheep mum.

Little Lamb loved being with Mum...

but Little Lamb could never lie still for long.

Skippety-hop!

Little Lamb skipped

and hopped

up...

down...

Baaa!

and all around. It made his mum laugh.

Skippety-hop!
Little Lamb **bounced**
as high as a bird,

and **boinged** right over a rabbit.

Skippety-hop!

Little Lamb **bumped** into a bee...

and frolicked after a **bobbing** butterfly.

Baaa! Baaa! Baaa!

As he went, Little Lamb heard his mum laughing,
"Baaa! Baaa! Baaa!", softer and softer,
and further and further away, until...

SPLASH!

Little Lamb fell right into the pond!

Now that was a surprise!

Little Lamb was soaked. He looked for his mum.
Where was she? He couldn't see her anywhere.

Little Lamb was lost.

"Have you seen my mum?" asked Little Lamb.

"Quack! Quack! Quack!"

went the ducks. "No, we haven't."

"**Mooo! Mooo!**" went the cows.

"No, we haven't either."

"Have you seen my mum?" asked Little Lamb.
"Woof! Woof!" went the farmer's dog.
"No, I haven't."

"Honk! Honk! Honk!"
went the geese.
"No, we haven't either."
But then...

Baaaaa!

Little Lamb turned to see Mum's soft woolly face,
her kind shining eyes and her gentle loving smile.

Then suddenly...

in she jumped!

SPLOOSH!

And in jumped Little Lamb too.

Little Lamb and Mum **ducked**

and **dived**

and **splashed** around the pond.

"Baaa!"
laughed Mum.

"Baaa!" laughed Little Lamb.
And after that...

Little Lamb was warm again in the sun
with his big sheep mum.

Notes for Parents and Teachers

- Before you read this book to a child, or children, look at the front cover and ask what they think the story is about.

- Read the story to the children, then ask them to read it to you, helping them with unfamiliar words and praising their efforts.

- Which is the children's favorite picture in the book? Discuss with them why they like it so much.

- Ask the children how they think Little Lamb felt when he realized he was lost. Discuss what children should do if they ever become lost.

- Little Lamb liked to move in different ways. How many ways can the children move? Which one do they like best? Ask the children to make up some words to describe the way they move.

- All the animals that Little Lamb asked made different noises. Make an animal noise from the book and ask the children which farm animal makes that sound. Can the children make their own farm animal noises? Do they know any other animal noises?

- Draw a picture of Little Lamb playing with his mother in the pond. Use paints, crayons, or pencils to make it colorful.

- Next time you visit the swimming pool with your child, pretend you are Little Lamb and his mother splashing in the pond. Try making different-size splashes, some small and gentle, others big and strong.

Editor: Alexandra Koken
Designer: Chris Fraser

Copyright © QEB Publishing, Inc. 2011

Published in the United States by
QEB Publishing, Inc.
3 Wrigley, Suite A
Irvine, CA 92618

www.qed-publishing.co.uk

Library of Congress Cataloging-in-Publication Data

Bedford, David, 1969-
 Little Lamb lost / David Bedford ; [illustrated by Karen Sapp].
   p. cm. -- (Storytime)
 Summary: When boisterous Little Lamb skippety-hops away from his mother and into a pond, he feels temporarily lost.
 ISBN 978-1-60992-030-2 (library bound)
 [1. Sheep--Fiction. 2. Animals--Infancy--Fiction. 3. Mother and child--Fiction. 4. Domestic animals--Fiction.] I. Sapp, Karen, ill. II. Title. III. Series.

 PZ7.B3817995Lil 2012
 [E]--dc22

                                              2010053309

ISBN 978 1 84835 547 7

Printed in China